PURSUIT OF POWER

A SECURITY DIRECTORATE SHORT STORY

ALEXANDRIA BLAELOCK

Also by Alexandria Blaelock

SHORT STORY COLLECTIONS
The Histories of Hayward Hall
Lovelorn, Lovestruck and Love at First Sight
Common or Garden Variety Heroes
Case Files of the Wilkinson Detective Agency
Unavoidable Fates
Christmas Travesties
Five Faces of Felicia Clarke
Little Place Called Home

FICTION
That Love Nonsense
Taipan vs Brown
The Ghost and Ms Cox
Friends Like That

MS BLAELOCK'S BOOKS
Stress Free Dinner Parties
Signature Wardrobe Planning
Holistic Personal Finance
Minimally Viable Housekeeping
Planning a Life Worth Living

A SELECTION OF AVAILABLE SHORT STORIES
Alma's Grace
Fate in Your Hands
Lady of the Looking Glass
Morning Star, Evening Star, Superstar
Secret Singer
Shining Star
Ship in a Bottle
Simone Says Hands in the Air
The Day the Schedule Broke

PURSUIT OF POWER

A SECURITY DIRECTORATE SHORT STORY

ALEXANDRIA BLAELOCK

BlueMere Books
MELBOURNE, AUSTRALIA

For permission requests, please contact
enquiries@bluemerebooks.com.

Ordering Information:
Discounts are available on quantity purchases. For details, contact orders@bluemerebooks.com.

Pursuit of Power/Alexandria Blaelock
paperback ISBN: 978-1-922744-88-3
digital ISBN: 978-1-922744-89-0

Book Layout © BookDesignTemplates.com
Cover Art © grandfailure/Depositphotos

PURSUIT OF POWER

It was a beautiful afternoon.

The sunlight glinted off the glass windows of the executive residential towers at exactly the right angle to blind anyone dumb enough to enter its hallowed sanctum.

The tall trees provided a canopy that protected the internal parkland area and koi pond from the heat, and the rhododendron shrubbery deflected the wind at ground level.

Rustic paved paths wended their way from corner to corner, providing secluded, private nooks for whatever the rich bastards got up to when no one was looking.

Though she felt sorry for the foreign maid who'd found her mistress's dead body sprawled by the pond.

Captain Tara Cline scowled at the dead woman at her feet. As soon as she'd rolled it over and seen its empty eye sockets, it was as much as she could do not to kick it.

"Well, well, well," came a voice from behind her, "if it isn't Captain Conjecture."

She closed her eyes and turned her face to the sun for a moment, before sighing and turning with a flick of her navy-blue uniform greatcoat.

Clicking her heels together, she nodded at him, "Captain Reprehensible. I wish I could say it was a pleasure to see you again."

Unfortunately, it was a pleasure to see his body; tall and slim, his uniform subtly tailored to enhance his physical attributes.

But for fuck's sake, when he opened his mouth and started talking, she just wanted to pull out her side arm and shoot him in the face.

He grinned, revealing neat and even straight white teeth.

"Then no doubt you'll be delighted to know that after eight eyeless corpses, I've been reassigned to assist you with your enquiries."

That was all she needed, the popular and well-connected Captain Max Wade hanging around and getting in the way.

Both Eugenics Programme successes, they'd passed Genomics Bureau post-natal testing around the same time. Attended, competed, and survived the State Academy of Cultural Regulation together, each with a useful genetic "superpower."

Back at the University of Civilisation, they'd dated for a nanosecond, during which she'd discovered his genetic "superpower" was the ability to get information out of people.

When he'd used it to discover hers was the ability to read what people saw in the last moments of their lives.

Through their cold, dead, sightless eyes.

And then he'd dumped her, presumably for someone with a power more advantageous to his long-term career and social position.

Not that the University permitted unsanctioned relationships, but you get up to a lot of stupid stuff at university.

And why bother asking for permission when you've no intention of making it last?

Despite the obvious suitability of their postings, it had irritated her to hear at the announcement ceremony they were both allocated to Investigations. Though happily, she hadn't seen hide nor hair of him in the last few years.

Only heard on the grapevine of his astronomical case closure rate.

She held out her hand, wiggling her fingers. "Orders please."

He held out the paper, but when she tried to pull it from his hand, he didn't let go.

Frowning, she met his eyes, and well aware that breaking his stare would seem like a sign of weakness, she gazed steadily at him.

After a few seconds, she felt him release his grip slightly and snatched the paper from his hands.

With an almost imperceptible winner's smile, she unfolded it to confirm what he'd said.

At eight dead, the bodies of Security Directorate officers were piling up. The lack of eyeballs to read was an inconvenience, but did Wade's appointment mean the Investigator General doubted her competence?

She refolded the paper precisely and tucked it in the breast pocket of her uniform jacket.

"I am ecstatic," she said, ramming her balled fists into her coat pockets, "with the official Directorate busybody on the case, I'm sure we'll wrap this nonsense up in no time at all."

He clutched his heart with two hands and staggered back a couple of steps. "I'm heartbroken you'd say such a thing. Especially when anyone can *see* you so clearly need my help."

Tara turned her back on him, and marched across to her investigations team and issued instructions, "the usual. Lieutenant Valdes; take the maid's statement, cordon off the area, do a local door knock for witnesses, and get the coroner's office and crime scene out."

Valdes nodded.

Max caught up and threw an arm around her shoulders, "so, Cline, what's the goss?"

Tara clenched her teeth. He'd been here less than five minutes, and already he was trying to undermine her credibility with her team.

Turning to face him, she twisted out from under his arm, without breaking it, much as she'd have liked to, and gestured at her lieutenant. "Captain Wade, this is Lieutenant Valdes. Valdes, Captain Wade is joining our investigation team today."

Valdes clicked his heels together and nodded before offering his hand, "Welcome to the team Captain Wade, I've heard a lot about you."

Max shook the offered hand and clapped Valdes on the shoulder, "as have I of you."

Valdes took on the look of a puppy blessed by a hearty, leg jerking belly rub. "I look forward to working with you. Can I show you the crime scene?"

Wade glanced at her. Somehow she managed an impassive face, and he nodded and allowed himself to be led away by the lieutenant.

She let her body relax a fraction, leaned on the nearby ruin of a shrine and pretended to leaf through her notebook while she thought through the implications of his appointment to her team.

At least she was still nominally in charge of the task force, which meant he was her resource, to do with what she thought was best.

Given the choice, he certainly wasn't the person she would've asked for, but his impressive case closure rate wasn't solely because of his interrogative powers.

He had a keen analytic mind, and she wasn't so petty as to send such a valuable resource packing when a fresh perspective might be useful.

A slight throat-clearing made her aware they had returned.

"Right. Valdes," she said, pocketing the notebook, "I'll take Captain Wade back to the office and bring him up to speed on the investigations so far. Let me know what you find."

He nodded in reply, "Ma'am."

And then to Max, "Sir."

And the sooner they got these cases solved, the sooner he'd be the hell out of her sight.

«« • »»

Back in the crowded, messy incident room, the first step was to knock on Major Kron's door to introduce Captain Wade and pass the orders on.

Naturally, the fat and lazy Kron needed a bit of time to fawn over the Superstar investigator.

She closed the door and left them to it. She'd already seen enough male bonding to last a lifetime.

She hung up her coat and cap as she returned to her desk, fortunately at the back of the room with five desks between her and Kron's Office, though sadly still facing it. On more than one occasion, she'd suddenly felt uncomfortable and looked up to see him staring at her in a way she couldn't interpret, but made her skin crawl nonetheless.

She logged into her computer, updated the initial victim and location details, and restarted the search for potential links. Then she printed pictures of the victim, dead and alive, as well as some of the scene.

With that out of the way, she lined up a new blank board alongside the other seven on the opposite wall, stuck the pictures to it and wrote out the pertinent victim details.

At this rate, she'd need to put the Supply Department on her speed dial.

The latest victim was a general's wife, so at least she wouldn't be required to carry out the Death Knock. That would be the Major's responsibility.

Ordinarily, she'd attend to observe the spouse's reaction, but this would be an excellent opportunity to put Wade to immediate use and get him out of her way.

The investigation would likely proceed on the assumption the General was innocent anyway, especially as his wife's appointment within the Directorate seemed in keeping with the context of the other murders.

Standing back far enough to see all the boards at once, she crossed her arms and tried to get her thoughts in enough of a semblance of order to brief Wade.

So far, all they'd identified was that the victims were Security Directorate officers, with no obvious defence wounds, and of course, the missing eyeballs.

No common appointments, ranks, genders, powers, location of work or motive.

No common *modus operandi* either, though it looked like the killer had targeted each victim in such a way they'd couldn't defend themselves.

And they'd scooped the eyeballs out with surgical precision, *post mortem.*

Of course, it was probably easier to remove the eyeballs after death (suggesting a single killer), but not for the first time, she wondered why the murderer didn't take them out first to disable the victim.

What did the killer hope to achieve from that?

Was it just a way to stop her from doing her thing?

Or a way to attract her attention and suspicion, to send the investigation into a dead end?

"Have you considered that the order of the murders is significant?" Wade startled her by asking.

She looked at him sharply, expecting mockery, but he was looking at the boards with his hands tucked casually in his trouser pockets.

"Why would I?"

"Ah, I guess you haven't needed to know before."

She frowned and made an impatient gesture. "What?"

"You know that rumour about how you can steal someone's powers if you kill them?"

She nodded her head sharply once.

"Under certain circumstances, it's true."

Tara growled with frustration, "I've got seven, I mean eight dead Directive officers and no one thought to share this with me?"

He shrugged, "perhaps as you should have been informed by now, they thought you knew."

"And that's something Kron should have passed on?"

"He's the most likely source, though it's possible he doesn't know either."

"How could they could promote you to Major and not know this?"

Wade said nothing, just looked at the floor and scrubbed at a mark on it with his toe.

"I see," she looked up at the ceiling, willing the tears of frustration away, "and now you swan in and solve the case in five minutes flat."

The ghost of a smile crossed his face. "I know I'm good, but I'm not that good."

"And what else is there that you're not telling me? You have a suspect, and it's someone highly placed."

Again, he avoided her eyes and didn't reply.

"This fucking day just gets better and better."

"Could be worse though. You're still in charge."

She snorted, "yeah, but for how long?"

"This case, at the very least."

"So, I've got eight murders to solve before the high-ranking killer strikes again."

"So now you're aware of the stakes. Let's get investigating."

She glanced at him, but couldn't detect any malicious intent.

"Fine," she gestured at the conference table in the centre of the incident room, "let's sit down and work this through.

"Aside from Officer status in the Directorate, we haven't identified any commonalities that suggest a reason these people were targeted."

She grabbed a bunch of files from her desk and tossed them on the table in front of him. He reached out to stop them from sliding off the other side.

"Am I authorised to share your new information with the team?"

He looked at her for a long moment, "if you think it would help the investigation."

She paced a few laps around the table while he flicked through the files and sorted them into the order of killing.

"Okay," walking past the boards, she picked up a marker and stopped beside the first, "let's not worry about sharing that detail right now, let's just focus on what the path of powers reveals. This is the first victim, Private Holly Devine. What's her power?"

"Find missing items."

"Right, the body in the library." Tara wrote that on the board and moved to the next, "victim two, Major Steven Smith.

"Power to manipulate metals."

"OK, Jewellery workshop. Next, victim three, Lieutenant John Peterson."

"Open doors."

Smiling, she snorted, "women's dorm."

He laughed, then she remembered they weren't friends and turned away.

"Private Sam Marlowe."

"Disrupt electronic communications."

"Propaganda Bureau studios. Then Captain Mike Colquhoun."

"Super strength."

"The gym. Followed by Private Jane Cooper."

"Levitation."

"Highpoint Tower. Next, Captain James Dalgleish."

"Setting fire."

"Local pool. And now we've Lieutenant Colonel Jennifer Frank."

"Melding glass."

"Astronomy lab."

They looked at each other, grinning.

Tara asked, "put it together, and what have you got?"

"Thief!" they said in unison.

Max held his hand up, and before she could stop herself, she'd slapped it.

Remembering he was probably after her job, she stepped back, turned away and looked again at the boards.

"So, if you're trying to become a better thief, what are you stealing, and what other powers are you going to need?"

He came to stand behind her, looking at the boards. "Something you have to find, get into a room with, that's so heavy you need help to move it, and then cover your traces."

She could almost feel his chest moving as he breathed, but the only way to break away from him was through him.

She turned to look at him, "like something in a locked case in a museum or gallery? Some kind of artefact you thought would give you the power to do something you wouldn't otherwise be able to do?"

"Like what, take over the Directorate?"

She turned back to the boards to let the idea sink in. Wasn't it a bit farfetched to think someone might try to steal an artefact to overthrow the Directorate?

"Given that information about powers is strictly controlled, how does our killer know who to target to gain the right powers?"

"We don't..." Wade started, "they don't know yet, but I think we can assume the killer is authorised to access that information."

"But isn't access strictly controlled and monitored?"

"Yes."

"Is it possible they have a power that helps them conceal their actions?"

"I suppose. It's also possible they've killed previously, and for whatever reason, those murders haven't been linked."

She rubbed the back of her neck, "so we should probably pull the files of all Directorate officer murders. But how far back?"

He shrugged one shoulder, "and how wide? When were you appointed to this task force, and on what basis?"

She frowned, "Wade, wouldn't it be easier to kill me than to keep scooping the eyeballs out?"

He just looked at her, expressionless.

"So not just another murder, but my own murder."

He nodded once in the affirmative.

"So, why are you really here?"

"Did you get a Notification of Union from the Bureau yet?"

"No, but I've been sleeping in the barracks lately, and haven't been home. How exactly is that relevant?"

He offered her a copy of an order from the Genomics Bureau.

Which announced the Directorate eugenics programme had done whatever it was it did, and paired her with him for a five-year contract. Dated June 15, with 21 days for appeal, all over and done with already.

Annoying.

Partly because she just didn't have time for a Union, and partly because it was him in particular.

She screwed up the paper and, as much as she wanted to drop-kick it into a nearby wastepaper basket, just let it fall to the floor as she turned on her heel, collected her hat and coat, and left the incident room.

«« • »»

Filled with murderous rage towards Wade, she paced the night streets silently, daring someone to attack her.

Though of course, only an insane person with a death wish was going to attack a uniformed Security Directorate Captain.

The longer she walked, the angrier she got, and the less of a bead she could get on someone trying to take over the Directorate.

After a point, she just wanted to kill something or someone and broke into the old barracks gym. Not that she didn't have easy access using the security code, but sometimes you needed to test your other skills.

Despite its scruffiness, she much preferred it to the new one, which was mainly inhabited by show-offs and poseurs, not people working seriously to maintain combat readiness.

How some people kept their postings was beyond her.

The old one, with its blood-stained walls and scratched up wood floor, was for serious work.

She threw her coat and hat aside, rolled up her sleeves, and wound some abandoned tape from the floor around her hands.

Then launched herself at a punching bag.

The air was acrid with stale sweat, and she had to keep tossing her head to stop her own from dripping in her eyes.

The sound of each blow echoed across the empty workout space and back again. She half expected the human-shaped punching bag to kneel and beg her to stop hitting it.

Maybe that was why someone else had pasted a cross shaped adhesive tape bandage on its head.

Having worked the first layer of brutal rage out of her system, she tried to think more logically about the murders, but Wade and her impending nuptials just kept getting in the way.

Perhaps she should give herself a break, towel down her face, drink some water and bloody try harder.

She unwound the tapes from her hands and grimaced at the bruises coming to the surface. Too late to put them back on. Her knuckles were already swelling.

Just one more annoyance in a day of nothing but annoyances.

She walked across to the water fountain, rinsed her mouth out and spat on the floor.

Given the pain in her jaw, she now knew she'd been clenching her teeth as well.

Bloody hell!

It'd only taken a couple of hours with him to stress her almost to breaking point.

Of all people, why did it have to be fucking Captain Max Wade?

Not that it was about him, or her, but the Directorate's breeding program.

Sometimes, the matches were so successful the parties renewed their contracts or even applied for permanence.

Though whether that was something to be envied was hard to know.

Did he request the Union, or was he really allocated by a random genetic match as the programme claimed?

Was it possible the Union was a way to provide 24-hour protection to an at-risk officer?

Was the Union even real?

Should she go home and check?

Mind you, he'd implied a senior officer could be responsible for the killings, so it was possible he was investigating her.

Or was he investigating higher up her chain?

His orders had seemed genuine, but where had he come from?

As she came to a halt, she realised she'd been pacing the floor.

Who did she know outside her chain who could discreetly check on that?

Alumni Association?

It had been less than a day since the transfer orders had been served, they wouldn't know to update their records yet, would they?

She did a quick circuit of the gym to make sure she really was alone, then broke into the office to use the phone. She flicked through the phone book until she found the listing and called the number.

It rang and rang and rang.

And just as she realised how late it was, and decided to hang up, someone answered the phone.

She spouted some nonsense about needing to contact him and received confirmation of her suspicions.

Bureau of Internal Investigations.

She hung up the phone, removed the evidence of her break and enter, and relocked the door as she left.

So, Wade was an II agent. Though that didn't get her any closer to knowing who was under investigation.

Or whether she could trust him.

She spun on one heel and launched a sidekick at the dummy.

It rocked back and forth on its stand, but didn't fight back.

Because it was immobile.

The missing piece of the puzzle!

The murderer could immobilise the victims. Before they knew they needed to fight back. And with the other stolen powers, it could be a man or woman.

Who could do whatever they wanted to because the victims couldn't fight back.

So Wade had helped her enquiries after all.

And now she had to tell him so he could cross-check his suspects.

She turned to walk away, but tripped over her feet and fell to the floor instead.

It wasn't until she tried to stand up she realised she couldn't move.

She tried again, harder, but remained uncomfortably prone on the floor.

"There's no point trying to move my dear Captain Cline, I have you pinned like a bug.

In fact, I think I might squash you like one too. I haven't done that before, and I think it might be fun."

She heard Major Kron laugh, and even worse, it sounded like he'd slapped his leg at his own joke.

How ridiculously melodramatic.

She couldn't even open her mouth to denounce him.

Couldn't even growl her frustration.

In any case, with the sensation of increasing weight on her back, it was getting harder to breathe, let alone speak.

"I was planning to let you live and take the fall, but once Wade arrived, I knew it wouldn't take the two of you long to figure out I've been withholding information crucial to the investigations."

If she could have grunted, she would, though a power kick to the balls would have disabled him momentarily as well as shut him the fuck up.

Not that Kron had ever seemed that competent, but then again, his role was more along the lines of managing the officers, their training, equipment, and welfare.

Not actually hands-on investigation.

As she gasped for air, she wondered for the first time how he'd achieved his command.

Did it involve another power he'd stolen from someone else?

Dammit, there were still so many questions, and it was looking like she wasn't going to get any answers.

Except with her senses on high alert, she thought she heard the faintest scrape of a service boot from one of the room's darkened corners.

Leaping to the conclusion someone was coming to her aid, she willed herself to stop fighting and relax enough to get a good spring when Kron's attention shifted.

Except, of course, the weight on her back was increasing, and as she relaxed, she felt several sharp pains in her chest signalling broken ribs.

She couldn't breathe, she couldn't move, she couldn't think.

She passed out.

«« • »»

She woke in pain, who knows how much later.

The white room was too bright, too cold, and smelled too strongly of an alcoholic antiseptic.

The hum of air conditioning and beeping machines was disorienting as well as deafening.

Her head hurt, her body hurt, and she was incredibly thirsty.

She groaned.

Almost instantly, someone beside her took her hand, and shortly after, she passed out again.

When she woke, the pain was almost bearable, the light dimmer and the air conditioner quieter. She could hear voices murmuring nearby.

Propped on a pile of pillows, she was more or less comfortable.

But still thirsty.

She tried to move her hand to the call button, but someone was holding it. In both of his hands, resting his head on them.

She tugged her hand. He didn't let go, but raised his tousled head to reveal Wade's bloodshot eyes. Along with his torn and bloodstained uniform shirt.

He looked at her silently for a moment, and she resisted the temptation to smooth down his hair.

He set her hand down on the crisp bed covers, picked up a glass of water from the table, adjusted the straw and brought it to her mouth to drink.

Water had never tasted so good.

She sipped and sipped, but when she tried to breathe at the same time, she started coughing, and the pain of it almost stopped her breathing altogether.

Wade quickly took her hand again, and the pain receded along with the need to cough.

Which was confusing, because his power was being a truth serum, so he shouldn't be able to take the pain away.

Except he'd mentioned when you killed a Directorate officer, it was possible to take their powers...

She wondered vaguely how many people he'd killed.

And that led to further speculation about how the powers stacked up, whether they ever cancelled each other out, if you could give them away or otherwise divest them.

And as she drifted back to sleep, whether this power was analgesic or anaesthetic.

The next time she woke, she was blessedly alone, with a call button in her hand.

She pushed the button.

A moment later, a pretty nurse bustled in, used a small torch to look into her eyes before taking her blood pressure, pulse, and temperature.

Tara let her complete her observations before asking, "how long have I been here?"

"Not long, only a couple of days."

A couple of days! There was too much to do to be out of contact for a couple of days.

"And when can I leave?"

"I'm afraid I can't tell you that, but I've paged the doctor, and he'll be along shortly."

Tara wanted to know exactly what was going on, but it seemed the nurse couldn't help her.

There was no point in getting agitated. That wouldn't get her answers any quicker, so she only nodded and let the nurse leave.

The next person she saw was a clean and starched Wade, in full uniform with new Major pips on his epaulettes.

She opened her mouth to make a sarcastic comment but, remembering he sat by her bed in bloodstained clothing, holding her hand, closed it after saying nothing.

Not to mention the impending union...

He tossed his peaked cap onto the table, hooked a chair closer with his foot and sat next to the bed, looking at her for what seemed like a long time.

"I assume you'd like an update?"

She nodded.

"The Academy initially assessed William Kron as a low-level generalist, but redirected him to specialist training after he showed some signs of talent. We now know he killed his first officer cadet and took her power during this time."

She nodded again.

"Despite his apparent laziness and lack of class attendance, he graduated from University with Honours. We've since tied him back to several other murders during this time."

She smiled tightly, so she wasn't the only one who'd noticed his general lack of ability.

"He progressed rapidly through the ranks, applying for and receiving promotional transfers around the time his superiors suspected his abilities weren't as exceptional as he'd portrayed them. And more than one colonel was happier to pass him on than to start disciplinary procedures."

She shook her head in disbelief.

"However, his last colonel notified Internal Investigations. We seeded the rumour of a mind-controlling ancient artefact, and we've been monitoring him closely since then."

"How was he able to kill so many officers while you were watching him?"

"We weren't aware of the extent of his murder spree until just recently. We classified several of the killings as accidental deaths, so we weren't tracking those powers."

"And by just recently, you mean until you killed him."

He looked at the floor but didn't deny it.

"So, since his first days at school, he more or less built up a massive grievance against the Directorate and decided he had to control it."

"Or perhaps even earlier, his parents signed him over to the State after their attempt to abort the foetus failed."

"I suppose some normals don't take it so well when they find they're carrying "superheroes"."

"No."

"So how do I come into the story?"

"We're not sure how you came to his attention, perhaps your ambition and exemplary service record. But we think at least some of his recent murders were intended to trigger the creation of a task force and get you assigned to it."

She shuddered as she grunted, and when the pain hit, sat up and grabbed her stomach.

He leaned across the bed, took one of her hands, and the pain receded.

So much better, "thanks for that."

She unsuccessfully attempted to withdraw her hand. "Um, how many powers do you have?"

"32."

"Are they all Kron's?"

"No."

"I see. And how long have you been licensed to kill Directorate officers?"

"I can't say."

She leaned back on her pillows and tried again to withdraw her hand.

"So. They assigned you to the task force to protect me, the Union was cover for staying close, and now you'll be moving on to another assignment?"

He laughed, "I'm not sorry to say that the Union is real, though it's postponed until you're up and about again."

She inspected him closely.

Just like her, he was a little older, maybe a little more mature. The creep of grey across his temples gave him a distinguished look.

He looked worried, and she tried not to smile.

"Stop," he said, you're embarrassing me."

They'd had some fun at Uni, and she really could do a lot worse than a Union with him.

Tara still wasn't entirely sure she was happy about the Union, but after another unsuccessful attempt to extract her hand, decided she objected slightly less.

THE END

ABOUT THE AUTHOR

Alexandria Blaelock writes stories, some of them for *Ellery Queen's Mystery Magazine* and *Pulphouse Fiction Magazine.*

She's also written five selfhelp books applying business techniques to personal matters like getting dressed, cleaning house, and feeding your friends.

She lives in a forest because she enjoys birdsong, and the smell of gum leaves. When not telecommuting to parallel universes from her Melbourne based imagination, she watches K-dramas, talks to animals, and drinks Campari. At the same time.

Discover more at www.alexandriablaelock.com.

IF YOU ENJOYED THIS STORY...

try the other Security Directorate stories

... or the collections

Why not try *The Ghost and Ms Cox*

Life interrupted

To say the letter was a surprise was an understatement. It arrived addressed to Miss Finlay Cox, which made the contents even more extraordinary.

Orphan Finn Cox inherits a cottage. Thinks it holds the key to her origins. Of course she takes a look. Who wouldn't?

But when she gets there, she gets more than she bargained for.

Is it friend, family or foe?